This book belongs to

_____

# Midnight Farm

by Carly Simon

Illustrated by David Delamare

Simon & Schuster
Books for Young Readers

My deepest appreciation to Wendy Ice
for her invaluable creative advice.
—D. D.

**SIMON & SCHUSTER BOOKS FOR YOUNG READERS**
An imprint of Simon & Schuster Children's Publishing Division
1230 Avenue of the Americas, New York, New York 10020
Copyright © 1997 by Carly Simon
Illustrations copyright © 1997 by David Delamare
SIMON & SCHUSTER BOOKS FOR YOUNG READERS
is a trademark of Simon & Schuster.
Book design by Paul Zakris
The text for this book is set in 21-point Windsor bold
The illustrations are rendered in acrylic
Printed and bound in the United States of America
First Edition
10 9 8 7 6 5 4 3 2 1
Library of Congress Cataloging-in-Publication Data
Simon, Carly.
Midnight farm / written by Carly Simon ; illustrated by David Delamare.
p.   cm.
Summary: Two brothers join a fantastical nighttime musical celebration
by the plants and animals on their farm on Martha's Vineyard.
ISBN 0-689-81237-X
[1. Night—Fiction.  2. Farm life—Fiction.  3. Stories in rhyme.]
I. Delamare, David, ill.  II. Title.
PZ8.3.S587Mi  1997
[E]—dc20   96-25568

The artwork was created with acrylic
inks using air brush application onto
a cold press illustration board.

To my godsons,
Jules and Noah

—C. S.

There's a farm that I know
Unlike any other farm—
As the sun goes down
The air gets warm
And the birds wake up
And the wildflowers bloom
And the sheep jitterbug
Under a round rolling moon.
And that's just the beginning . . .
Now the rest will unfold. . . .
It was the summer Noah and I
Turned five years old.

One night in July
We woke to hoots and howls—
It sounded nothing like a nightingale
Nothing like an owl.
We looked out the window
And the sea was very calm
But the joint was jumping
On our Martha's Vineyard farm.
Just when you'd expect
Every living thing to doze
Vegetables and flowers
Were putting on their clothes.

In our pajamas
We left the house
And were led to the yard
By a little field mouse.
In a squeaky clear voice
She said, "Kids are allowed
You'll be rather amused
You'll be part of the crowd."
As we walked through the garden
The onions and the peas
Did a jig just to welcome
My twin brother and me.

A nd while nothing can sleep

Like a cantaloupe can

Nocturnal snoozing

Was not part of the plan.

A flock of flamingoes

Woke the dear melon

With their chattering, bickering

Yowlin' and yellin'.

They were arguing over

Whose beak was longer

Whose pink was pinker

And whose legs were stronger.

The cantaloupe split open

From laughing so hard

And animals joined in

All over the yard.

They came from the barn
And from the neat flower beds
And from those winding little furrows
Where moles poke their heads.
Raccoons checked their hairdos
Mosquitoes revved their whines
While weeds, usually messy,
Formed tidy straight lines.
"Looks like the songs
Are about to begin,"
The field mouse informed us
As she raised her mandolin.
"Come meet the tulip
Who conducts the midnight choir
He's an old fuddy-duddy
But he's about to retire."

A colt and a kitten
And a new baby lamb
Wobbled into the yard
Just in time for the jam
And an old apple tree
Who had to bend pretty far
Strummed a little strum
On a driftwood guitar.
A cabbage whose feet
Looked a lot like his face
Played the coolest of notes
On a beetlebung bass
While a moth from Menemsha
And a gull from West Chop
Beat time with their wings
On a scrub oak tree top.

As if by magic
A goat with a goatee
Gave a flute and an oboe
To Noah and me.
There was nothing to do
But pucker and blow—
It knocked the socks off a cricket
And the pants off a crow.
All eyes were upon us
As the tulip turned 'round,
He struck his baton
Quite hard on the ground:
"If you're going to play
Please play the same song
I cannot hear the hymn
When your notes are all wrong."

Then he handed us music
On sycamore leaves
And suddenly in buzzed
A great swarm of bees.
They surrounded us, filling in
"Ooohs" and then "ahhhs"
And an audience of cows
Went wild with applause.
This woke up the pond
First the fish then the frogs
Who splashed sparkling water
On a few of the hogs
(Or pigs as we call them)
And they ran just like elves
Stealing a piece of the night
For themselves.

J oining in on the fun
A fox on a tractor
Wore a hat with a brim
Like a Hollywood actor.
He tried to round up the pigs
Like some rough cowboy dude
But it frightened the roses
And the bees thought it rude.
Noah feared we'd get stung
The queen bee looked so mean
When we ran we got tangled
In her wide crinoline.

So the tulip conductor

Became very cross.

He shouted, "Boys will be boys

But I am the boss!

Go back to the house

Get back into bed."

His face, once just rosy,

Turned fire engine red.

Poor tulip conductor

He was trying so hard

"Be professionals!" he shouted

And that cracked up the yard.

The queen laughed so much

That her crinoline ripped

And Noah and I took a fall

And then flipped . . .

We rolled over and over
And down a great hill
And bumped into a turtle
Heating pearls on a grill.
"What are you doing?"
I couldn't help but ask.
The turtle looked giddy
As he explained his strange task:
"You see, when they're warm
They float toward the moon
Then rain down on the farm
Making everything swoon
And sleep shortly follows
The magic will be over
And I'll crawl very slowly
Back under my cover."

Just then a dolphin
With silver-green eyes
Jumped out of the ocean
And continued to rise.
As we gazed at the sky
The wind caught the pearls
And I knew that it signaled
A change in the world.
Noah started to cry
He didn't want it to end
He said that the turtle
Was going to be his best friend.
As the pearls turned to mist
It all seemed so weird
We looked back at the turtle
But he'd just disappeared.

We walked back up the hill
And the bees were all gone
The tulip conductor
Had dropped his baton.
The pigs were a cluster
Of pink in their box
And no tracks from the tractor
No trace of the fox.
The cantaloupe slept
Like the inventor of sleep
And the cows and the kittens
Snored alongside the sheep.
The moth and the gull
Snuggled close to a wren
And the old apple tree
Stood straight up again.

The moon sat right down
Like a schooner at sea
The morning wouldn't wait
For Noah and me.
Just the mouse was still waiting
As mice often wait
To show us to the door
Saying, "Gee, it got late,
But really it's early
I guess they're one and the same,
Good night little boys
I'm glad that you came."
All we could hear
Was a nightingale's song
Our island farm was wrapped
In a mist a mile long.

As we drifted to sleep
We knew there'd be more
We'd never know when
Or how, or what for.
But we knew something would wake us
Again one late night
And I'm so happy to tell you,
Yes . . .
we
were
right.